Handsta...

Baking Around the World
by Yvette Garfield

Designed by Kyumi Christensen

Published by Handstand Kids, LLC
Printed in China by Amica Inc., 02/18/2012
ISBN: 978-0-9847476-0-3

By Yvette Garfield
Illustrated & Designed by Kyumi Christensen
Character and Illustration Design by Kim DeRose
Recipes Edited and Developed by Yvette Garfield
Editing by Tracy Sway

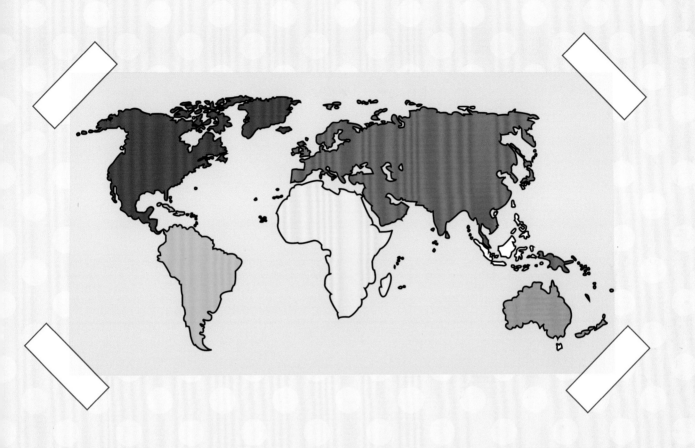

This Book Belongs To:

Sofia Flores

Dedication

This book is dedicated to my mother, who taught all the students at my elementary school to bake cupcakes in a cone.

Special Thanks

Many thanks to Catherine McCord, Emily Dubner and Arleen Scavone for their recipe contributions. Catherine's Red Velvety Beet Cupcakes cannot be topped. Emily's whoopie pies are the greatest. And Arleen's PB&J Cupcakes, Carrot Walnut cupcakes and Pumpkin Bread Pudding are just about perfect.

I am also grateful to Tracy Sway, Ruth Lerdahl and Kyumi Christensen for their many talents and hard work in creating this book from scratch.

Table of Contents

Foreword

Sharing and enjoying home-made baked goodies is the true meaning of "comfort" in food and life.

I grew up in a rural low-income area in the South Park annex of Santa Rosa, California. My father was a truck driver carrying rock and gravel; my mom didn't drive, but, a true Italian homemaker, she was a favorite among our local bus drivers. My sister and brother are both older and we remain close as family today. My mom shopped on a $5 bill a day most days, although some days weren't as generous. My grandma, Nanny, lived with us throughout my childhood. We spent many hours each day in the kitchen preparing meals for the table. No matter what, mom always insisted on having the best staples: flour, sugar, whole milk and, of course, real butter! I honestly don't think I tasted margarine until adulthood.

My sister and I were always in charge of desserts—cakes, breads, cookies—nothing fancy, but there was always something sweet wrapped up and ready to be shared with a cup of tea or a glass of milk. We had a wood-burning stove with an oven door that had to be held closed with a wooden stick. I was never sure of the temperature inside, but my cakes and pies came out fine! My sister was known in family circles for her fruitcake and banana-walnut bread. My mom always wore an apron and my sister and I use to make aprons for her each Mothers' Day. Today, I love wearing special aprons for holidays as I bake in my home kitchen with my husband and three children—it's a bit less formal than our chef coats at Sweet Arleen's bakery. I think that's why I love the Handstand Kids aprons; they remind me of being at home baking with my family, both then and now. Donning that apron means, "I'm ready to preheat the ovens!"

While I was not professionally trained, I majored in Home Economics throughout my school years. My most influential teacher was Mrs. Morse. She was an ultimate planner, very exact. I learned to set all ingredients out in order of their use, measured exactly according to the recipe. I learned to leave my cracked eggs out on the counter, or to only remove from the refrigerator the exact number of eggs needed for the recipe, so I would never mistake how many eggs I've put in the batter. That lesson paid off during my two-time win on Cupcake Wars! Mrs. Morse was strict with a purpose. I loved her, and I respected her. I've brought many of the disciplines I learned from her to Sweet Arleen's today. Our cupcakes and bread puddings must be perfect and exact every day.

I'd like to share this message with all of the Handstand Kids readers: No matter how old you are, learning to read and follow recipes, cherish your cook books, and share your baking experiments with your friends and family is a meaningful and powerful ritual. I've baked all my life and there is nothing I love more than planning and preparing my next comforting creation.

Enjoy!

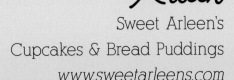

Arleen

Sweet Arleen's
Cupcakes & Bread Puddings
www.sweetarleens.com

Utensils:

Baking Pan	Cutting Board	Baking Sheet	Cupcake Sheet

Electric Mixer	Ladle	Measuring Cups	Measuring Spoons

Mixing Bowls (Large, Medium, Small)	Mitt	Pastry Brush	Rolling Pin

Wooden Spoon	Whisk	Spoon	Spatula

Ingredients:

Agave Nectar	Apple	Baking Soda	Baking Powder	Brown Sugar

Butter	Beet	Carrot	Chocolate Chips	Chocolate
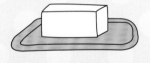				

Cinnamon	Cream Cheese	Eggs	Flour	Honey
		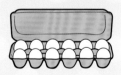		

Jam	Lemon Juice	Milk	Nuts (Walnuts & Almonds)	Peanut Butter

Salt	Strawberry	Sugar	Vanilla	Vegetable Oil

Recipe Levels: Cupcakes

Look for the cupcakes at the top of each recipe to determine the recipe's level of difficulty. Each recipe is ranked between levels 1 and 4; more cupcakes means that more adult help is encouraged.

Remember, an adult supervisor must be in the kitchen at all times!

 1 Cupcake – Level 1 means this is a basic recipe and that you can do most of the steps yourself.

 2 Cupcakes – Level 2 means that the recipe is a little bit harder and there are some steps that an adult will need to help you with.

 3 Cupcakes – Level 3 means that an adult will need to handle certain steps.

 4 Cupcakes – Level 4 means that an adult will need to help you with the entire recipe.

Stir it Up!

Congratulations on becoming a baker! It's tons of fun to bake and eat these tasty treats, but you can also use them to brighten someone else's day. Try making these recipes for your friends and family. Your baking skills can also be used to help those in need. Local charities and food banks may welcome food donations and youth volunteers; check the Handstand Kids website for volunteer opportunities at www.handstandkids.com. Using your new cooking skills in these ways can help change the world, so lets get started!

Introduction

Welcome to the Handstand Kids Baking Around the World Cookbook. Baking is a fun and hands-on way to learn about different cultures. When you learn to cook recipes from another country, you open your kitchen to a world of experiences. While people around the world have many differences, they all enjoy delicious foods and recipes that are special to their region.

The Handstand Kids (Ari, Felix, Gabby, Izzy and Marvin) can't wait to introduce you to baking recipes and desserts from around the world! Each recipe in this book includes an alternative suggestion to encourage you to add your own creativity and favorite flavors to the recipe. An adult supervisor must be present in the kitchen at all times to assist kid chefs, especially when cooking over the stove or using sharp objects. Adult supervision will ensure that kid chefs are always safe.

It is my intention that the Handstand Kids cookbook series will provide a fun and delicious way to learn about the world and inspire you to make it a better place. So join the Handstand Kids as they travel the world, one recipe at a time!

Happy Cooking,

Yvette Garfield

Meet The

IZZY

Birthday July 5

Hey! I'm Izzy and I'm ten and a half years old. Everyone says I am the pickiest eater, but I love spaghetti and chocolate chip cookies. I am excited to try new types of cookies from different countries.

My sister has diabetes, which means she can't eat sugar. So I want to find some recipes for tasty sugar-free treats that she can enjoy too.

FELIX

Birthday February 8

I'm Felix and I am nine years old. I love taking cooking classes at my school. I am a vegetarian, which means that I don't eat any meat. My whole family is vegetarian and we love baking together for holidays. Each year my mom makes the most delicious apple cinnamon cake.

It will be so fun to experiment with making cupcakes in a cone, like ice cream! I will invite my friends to come over to share them with me. Each friend can get creative and decorate his or her own!

Handstand Kids

GABBY

Birthday October 7

Hi! I'm Gabby and I am eleven years old. My favorite hobby is learning new languages. So far I can speak three languages pretty well: English, Spanish and Farsi. I absolutely love learning new words and I hope that one day I can speak to people around the world in their native languages. I know that's ambitious, but I am starting young.

I really love to bake and I can't wait to learn about baking around the world. It will be awesome to make international treats for my friends. I'm also going to bake cupcakes for my dad's birthday!

MARVIN

Birthday April 19

Hi! I'm Marvin and I want to be a chef when I grow up. I'm only ten so I still have a lot to learn about cooking. My mom teaches me recipes from all the cool places she has traveled. So far my favorite recipe is for the biscotti cookies from Italy. So crunchy!

When I grow up I want to have a restaurant where I can bake and serve desserts from around the world.

ARI

Birthday December 17

My name is Ari and I am eight years old. I love to eat all kinds of foods! My family thinks I am funny because I will try almost any food.

I am so excited to learn to bake so I can host my very own bake sale! I think my new baking skills will help me to raise money for cool organizations. My favorite food of all time is cookies and I can't wait to try different cookies from around the world. Yum!

All Kids

Love ...

Cupcakes!

Peanut Butter & Jelly Cupcakes with Peanut Butter Frosting

Peanut Butter & Jelly Cupcakes

Ingredients

1 ¾ cups all-purpose flour

2 ¼ teaspoons baking powder

½ teaspoon salt

¼ teaspoon baking soda

½ cup butter (1 stick),
softened at room temperature

1 ¾ cups granulated sugar

¾ cup creamy peanut butter

3 eggs

¼ cup sour cream

½ teaspoon vanilla extract

¼ cup vegetable oil

½ cup buttermilk

1 jar of strawberry jam

Tools

Measuring cups

Measuring spoons

3 large bowls

Whisk

Electric mixer or hand mixer

Rubber spatula

Spoon

Lined cupcake pans or baking cups

Melon baller

Alternative

For those with nut allergies,
try this recipe with sunflower
seed butter. For a healthier
alternative, use strawberry
jam as frosting.

Instructions

1. Preheat oven to 350 degrees.

2. Place the flour, baking powder, salt
   and baking soda in a large bowl and
   whisk to combine, set aside.

3. Place the softened butter and sugar
   in another large bowl and beat with
   an electric mixer on a low speed
   until smooth.

4. Add peanut butter to the bowl with
   the butter and sugar and mix on low
   speed until combined.

5. Add one egg and mix to combine.
   Repeat with remaining 2 eggs,
   mixing after each to combine before
   adding the next.

6. In another large bowl, whisk
   together the sour cream, vanilla
   extract, oil and buttermilk,
   set aside.

7. Add half of the dry flour mixture to
   the bowl with the butter. Mix on low
   speed until combined.

8. Add the sour cream mixture to the
   bowl and mix until combined.

9. Using rubber spatula, scrape
   down sides to make sure there are
   no lumps.

10. Add remaining flour mixture and
    mix until smooth.

11. Use a spoon to scoop the mixture
    into 20 lined cupcake pans or
    baking cups.

12. Bake cupcakes for approximately 20
    minutes until golden brown, and let
    cool at room temperature.

13. Once cooled, use the melon baller to
    gently scoop out a small piece from
    the center of each cupcake.

14. Fill the holes with the strawberry
    jam. Cover tops of cupcakes with
    Peanut Butter Frosting.

Peanut Butter Frosting

Ingredients

1 cup powdered sugar

1 cup creamy peanut butter

5 tablespoons butter, softened at
room temperature

¾ teaspoon vanilla extract

¼ teaspoon salt

⅓ cup heavy cream

Tools

Measuring cups

Measuring spoons

Large bowl

Electric mixer or hand mixer

Sifter

Rubber spatula

Instructions

1. Place the butter, vanilla,
   salt and peanut butter in a
   large bowl and beat with an
   electric mixer or hand mixer
   until combined.

2. Use the sifter to place
   powdered sugar into the
   large bowl. Beat with mixer
   until there are no lumps.

3. Use the rubber spatula
   to scrape the sides of
   bowl, stirring any lumps
   until smooth.

4. Slowly mix in heavy
   cream until just combined.
   If you stir the icing too
   much, it will turn grainy
   and separate.

5. Spread frosting on cupcakes
   and serve!

Red Velvety Beet Cupcakes with Red Beet Cream Cheese Frosting

Red Velvety Beet Cupcakes

Ingredients

2 large red beets

2 cups all-purpose flour

2 teaspoon baking powder

½ teaspoon baking soda

½ teaspoon salt

2 large eggs

1 cup milk

½ cup honey

⅓ cup vegetable or canola oil

2 teaspoons vanilla extract

Tools

Knife

Aluminum foil

Oven mitts

Food processor or blender

Measuring cups

Measuring spoons

Sifter

2 mixing bowls

2 small bowls

Rubber spatula

Alternative

Bake mixture in a cake pan for 35 minutes to make a red velvet cake.

Instructions

1. Preheat oven to 400 degrees.

2. Cut off greens and tail of beets, wash them and then wrap each beet in foil to make a closed package.

3. Place beet packages in the oven for 1 hour. Remove using oven mitts and let cool.

4. Once cooled, remove beets from foil and peel off beet skin using a plastic bag on your hand as a glove.

5. Place beets in food processor or blender and puree until smooth. Divide beet puree evenly into 2 small bowls.

6. Lower the oven temperature to 350 degrees.

7. Sift the flour, baking powder, baking soda and salt into a mixing bowl.

8. Place the eggs, milk, honey, oil and vanilla in a separate bowl and stir with spatula to combine.

9. Slowly add the dry ingredients into the wet and stir to combine.

10. Pour batter into lined cupcake pans or baking cups (approximately ⅓ cup batter per cupcake) and bake for 25 minutes.

11. Remove and let cool at room temperature, then top with Red Beet Cream Cheese Frosting.

Red Beet Cream Cheese Frosting

(Makes about 2 Cups)

Ingredients

1 cup cream cheese, softened at room temperature

½ cup unsalted butter (1 stick), softened at room temperature

½ cup powdered sugar

1 teaspoon vanilla

Remaining beet puree from previous recipe

Tools

Electric or hand mixer

Large bowl

Frosting spreader or spoon

Instructions

1. Place all the ingredients in a bowl and beat with an electric mixer on medium to high speed until fluffy.

2. Spread frosting on cupcakes and serve!

Carrot Walnut Cupcakes with Cream Cheese Frosting

Carrot Walnut Cupcakes

Ingredients

½ cup granulated sugar

½ cup dark brown sugar

2 eggs

¼ cup vegetable oil

1 cup all-purpose flour

½ teaspoon baking soda

½ teaspoon salt

1 teaspoon cinnamon

1 ¼ cups shredded carrots

¼ cup chopped walnuts

Tools

Measuring cups

Measuring spoons

Whisk

Mixing bowl

Rubber spatula

Lined cupcake pans or baking cups

Alternative

Make carrot cake by placing the batter in a square baking pan and baking for 40 to 45 minutes.

Instructions

1. Preheat oven to 350 degrees.

2. Whisk the sugars, eggs and oil together in a large mixing bowl.

3. Add the flour, baking soda, salt and cinnamon to the sugar mixture and whisk until combined.

4. Use spatula to fold in carrots and walnuts.

5. Spoon batter into the lined cupcake pans or baking cups and bake for 20 minutes.

6. Remove and let cool at room temperature, then top with Cream Cheese Frosting.

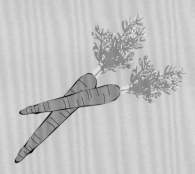

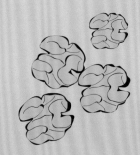

Cream Cheese Frosting

Ingredients

1 cup cream cheese, softened at room temperature

4 tablespoons unsalted butter

2 tablespoons sour cream

1 ½ teaspoons vanilla

3 cups powdered sugar

Tools

Mixing bowl

Electric mixer or hand mixer

Sifter

Rubber spatula

Measuring cups

Measuring spoons

Instructions

1. Place cream cheese in mixing bowl. Beat with electric mixer on low speed until smooth.

2. Scrape down the sides of bowl with spatula and beat to make sure there are no lumps.

3. Add softened butter and beat on low speed until smooth. Add sour cream and beat on low speed until smooth.

4. Turn off mixer and slowly add powdered sugar to the bowl.

5. Add vanilla and beat again on low speed until smooth.

6. Spread frosting on cupcakes and serve.

Level  🧁🧁🧁

Makes: About 20 Cupcakes

Vanilla Cupcakes in a Cone

Ingredients

1 ½ cups all-purpose flour

1 ½ teaspoons baking powder

½ teaspoon salt

½ cup unsalted butter, softened

½ cup sugar

2 large eggs

¼ cup unsweetened applesauce

¼ cup low-fat milk

1 teaspoon vanilla extract

20 standard ice cream cones (with flat bottoms)

Sundae toppings (sprinkles, chocolate sauce, cherries)

Tools

Measuring cups

Measuring spoons

Whisk

2 mixing bowls

Electric or hand mixer

Rubber spatula

Baking sheet

Alternative

Use different toppings to decorate for a birthday party and put a candle in a cupcake for the lucky birthday kid.

Instructions

1. Preheat oven to 350 degrees.

2. Whisk the flour, baking powder and salt in a bowl and set aside.

3. Place the butter and sugar in another mixing bowl and beat with an electric mixer on medium-high speed for 2 minutes or until light and fluffy.

4. Add one egg and beat on low speed to combine. Add the second egg and vanilla and beat on low speed to combine.

5. Slowly add some of the flour mixture and then some of the milk and beat until just combined. Then add the rest of the flour and milk, scraping down the sides of the bowl with a rubber spatula and beating until just combined.

6. Pour the batter into the ice cream cones, just up to the stem of the cone, as the batter will rise.

7. Place the cones on a baking sheet and carefully place in the oven for approximately 20 minutes.

8. Let the cones cool for 15 minutes and then frost with Butter Cream Frosting and top with sprinkles, chocolate sauce, and a cherry to look like an ice cream sundae!

Butter Cream Frosting

(Makes about 1 Cup)

Ingredients

½ cup cream cheese, softened at room temperature

4 tablespoons butter, softened at room temperature

1 cup powdered sugar

1 teaspoon vanilla extract

Tools

Measuring cups

Measuring spoons

Electric or hand mixer

Mixing bowl

Instructions

1. Place the cream cheese and butter in a mixing bowl and beat with an electric mixer on low to medium speed for 30 seconds.

2. Add the powdered sugar and vanilla and continue to beat for one minute or until frosting is smooth and creamy.

3. Spread the frosting on the cupcakes then decorate with chocolate sauce, sprinkles and a cherry to look like sundae in a cone.

How the Cookie Crumbles...

Ingredients

1 cup unsalted butter, softened at room temperature

1 cup brown sugar, packed

1 cup oats (quick, uncooked)

½ cup white sugar

2 large eggs, at room temperature

1 tablespoon vanilla extract

1 cup all-purpose flour

1 ¼ cup whole wheat flour

1 teaspoon baking soda

½ teaspoon salt

1 cup semi-sweet chocolate chips

½ teaspoon cinnamon

½ teaspoon salt

Tools

Measuring cups

Measuring spoons

Electric mixer

Mixing bowl

Wooden spoon

Baking sheet

Parchment paper

Alternative

Try replacing the white sugar with ¼ cup of honey or agave nectar.

Instructions

1. Preheat oven to 375 degrees.

2. Cream the butter and sugar in a standing mixer (or in a bowl using a hand mixer) for 5 minutes until light and fluffy.

3. Add the eggs one at a time, mixing after each addition. Add vanilla extract and mix for 1 minute.

4. Combine the white flour, whole wheat flour, baking soda and salt in a bowl and slowly incorporate into the butter and egg mixture.

5. Mix until combined then pour in the chocolate chips and stir.

6. Using a miniature ice cream scooper or tablespoon measure, scoop dough onto a parchment-lined baking sheet.

7. Bake for 15 minutes and remove from oven. Let cookies cool on the baking sheet and place on a cooling rack.

Ingredients

½ cup unsalted butter, softened at room temperature

½ cup powdered sugar

¼ teaspoon ground nutmeg

¼ teaspoon ground cardamom

1 cup all-purpose flour

¼ teaspoon baking powder

¼ teaspoon salt

¼ cup milk

Handful of almonds, cashews or shelled pistachios

Tools

Measuring cups

Measuring spoons

Mixing bowls

Wooden spoon

Sifter

Plastic wrap

Baking sheet

Parchment paper

Instructions

1. Preheat oven to 350 degrees.

2. Place the softened butter and powdered sugar in a mixing bowl and combine until mixture is light and creamy.

3. Add the nutmeg and cardamom and mix well.

4. In a separate bowl, sift flour, baking powder and salt. Mix butter with the flour mixture to form a soft dough.

5. Wrap dough in plastic wrap and let rest for 15 minutes.

6. Knead the dough again, make small balls approximately 1 inch in diameter and press each between your palms to flatten. Smooth out the edges and place on parchment paper-lined baking sheet, leaving space between as they will spread while baking.

7. Dip the nuts into milk and place one or two on top of each cookie.

8. Bake cookies for 15 minutes or until slightly golden, remove and let cool.

Alternative

Try making an Indian cookie sandwich. Place a scoop of mango ice cream between two Nan Khatai. Enjoy!

Raspberry Rugelach Twists

Ingredients

½ cup unsalted butter, softened at room temperature

½ cup cream cheese, softened at room temperature

½ teaspoon vanilla extract

1 cup all-purpose flour

1 large egg mixed with 1 tablespoon water

¼ cup raspberry or strawberry preserves

½ cup miniature chocolate chips

Tools

Measuring cups

Measuring spoons

Food processor or standing mixer

Plastic wrap

Pizza cutter or knife

Pastry brush

Alternative

Try filling the rugelach with chopped walnuts and raisins.

Instructions

1. Preheat the oven to 350 degrees. Place the butter, cream cheese and vanilla in a food processor or standing mixer and mix until combined.

2. Slowly add the flour, little by little until just combined.

3. Divide the dough into 2 balls, wrap each with plastic wrap and refrigerate for 1 hour.

4. On a lightly floured surface, roll each dough ball into a 9-inch round and cut each into 12 equal wedges, like a pizza pie, using a pizza cutter or knife.

5. Before separating the wedges, evenly spread the rounds with the preserves.

6. Sprinkle chocolate chips on top and press them down gently to adhere to the dough.

7. Starting with the wide end of a wedge, roll into a spiral. Repeat with each other wedge.

8. Place the rolled cookies on a baking sheet with the tip pointing down and brush with egg wash.

9. Bake for 20 minutes or until golden. Remove and enjoy!

Bella Biscotti Cookies

Ingredients

2 ½ cups flour

¾ teaspoon salt

2 teaspoons baking powder

1 ½ cups sugar

5 eggs

1 teaspoon vanilla extract

½ cup sliced almonds

½ cup miniature chocolate chips

1 teaspoon cinnamon

1 tablespoon butter

Tools

Baking sheet

Cutting board

Large bowl

Measuring cup and spoon

Serrated knife

Small bowl

Wooden spoon

Pastry brush

Alternative

Melt 1 cup chocolate chips in the microwave for one minute and dip the ends of the cooled biscotti into the mixture. Refrigerate dipped biscotti for 1 hour and enjoy.

Instructions

1. Preheat the oven to 375 degrees.

2. Grease a large baking sheet with a light coat of butter and then sprinkle the sheet with flour.

3. Mix the flour, sugar, baking powder and salt together in the large bowl and make a hole in the middle of the mixture.

4. Add 4 eggs, cinnamon, and vanilla into the hole and use the wooden spoon to stir it thoroughly.

5. Add the almonds and chocolate chips evenly throughout the dough and use your hands to shape the dough into 2 logs.

6. Place each log onto the baking sheet, leaving 4 inches between the edges and the dough.

7. Beat 1 egg in the small bowl and use the pastry brush to coat the logs with the egg.

8. Bake the logs in the oven for 15 minutes, until golden brown.

9. Allow the logs to cool for 10 minutes and place them on the cutting board and cut them diagonally into 2 inch slices.

10. Arrange the slices back onto the baking sheet so that the cut sides are facing up and bake for another 5 minutes.

11. Cool the slices and bite into the crunchy goodness!

It's a Piece of Cake!

Traditional Mexican Chocolate Cake

Ingredients

½ cup butter (1 stick), softened at room temperature

1 cup granulated sugar

1 teaspoon vanilla extract

2 eggs

6 ounces semi-sweet chocolate

2 teaspoons ground cinnamon

¼ teaspoon salt

1 teaspoon baking soda

2 cups all-purpose flour

1 cup milk

1 cup water

1 teaspoon powdered sugar

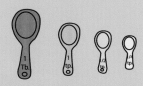

Tools

Measuring cups

Measuring spoons

2 large bowls

Small microwave-safe bowl

Electric mixer

Sifter

Whisk

9 x 13-inch baking pan

Alternative

Add in a handful of chopped pecans to the batter before pouring into the baking pan.

Instructions

1. Preheat oven to 350 degrees. Lightly grease baking pan with butter or cooking spray.

2. Place the butter and sugar in a large bowl and beat with an electric mixer.

3. Add one egg and beat on low speed to combine. Add the second egg and vanilla and beat on low speed to combine.

4. Chop the chocolate into pieces and place in a small microwave-safe bowl. Melt chocolate by heating in the microwave for 30 seconds at a time and stirring until completely melted. Add the chocolate to the mixing bowl and beat to combine.

5. Sift the cinnamon, salt, baking soda and flour into a large bowl and whisk to combine.

6. Slowly add some of the flour mixture to the chocolate mixture, and then some of the milk, and beat until just combined. Then add the rest of the flour mixture and milk, scraping down the sides of the bowl with a rubber spatula and beating until just combined.

7. Pour the mixture into the baking pan and bake for 30 minutes or until a toothpick inserted into the center comes out clean.

8. Place on a wire rack to cool for 15 minutes.

9. Dust lightly with cinnamon and confectioner's sugar, using the sifter to distribute evenly. Place on a cake plate and serve.

Korean Sweet Potato Cake

Korean Sweet Potato Cake

Ingredients

1 medium sweet potato

1 cup butter (2 sticks), softened at room temperature

⅔ cup granulated sugar

⅔ cup brown sugar

3 eggs

1 teaspoon vanilla extract

2 cups all-purpose flour, plus more for flouring the pans

1 cup cake flour

1 tablespoon baking powder

1 teaspoon salt

1 ½ cups low-fat milk

⅓ cup maple syrup

Tools

Measuring cups

Measuring spoons

Fork

Sifter

3 large mixing bowls

Whisk

Wooden spoon

Rubber spatula

2 9-inch round cake pans

Alternative

Substitute whole wheat flour for the all-purpose flour for a healthier cake.

Instructions

1. Preheat oven to 350 degrees. Grease the baking pan with butter, then sprinkle flour in the pan and tap the sides to spread it around evenly.

2. Poke the sweet potato with a fork several times and place in the oven for 45 minutes. Remove using oven mitts and let cool.

3. Once cooled, peel and discard the skin from the sweet potato, place in a large bowl and mash it with a fork until soft.

4. Add the milk and maple syrup to the mashed sweet potato and stir to combine. Set aside.

5. Place the flours, baking powder and salt in another large bowl and whisk to combine. Set aside.

6. Place the butter and sugars in another large bowl and beat with an electric mixer on a low speed until smooth.

7. Add the vanilla and eggs, one at a time, beating to mix completely after each addition. Beat egg and butter mixture on medium speed until very light in color, about 4 minutes.

8. When the butter mixture is light and fluffy, add ⅓ of the flour mixture and beat to combine. Add ½ of the sweet potato mixture and beat to combine.

9. Add another ⅓ of the flour mixture and the rest of the sweet potato mixture and beat to combine.

10. Add the rest of the flour mixture and beat, scraping down the sides of the bowl to fully combine.

11. Pour the batter evenly into the cake pans. Tap the pans lightly on the counter to remove any air bubbles. Bake for 45 minutes, until a toothpick inserted in the center comes out clean

12. Cool cakes in their pans for 15 minutes, then turn out on to wire racks to cool completely. Frost with Butter Cream Frosting.

Butter Cream Frosting

(Makes about 4 Cups)

Ingredients

1 ½ cups cream cheese, softened at room temperature

¾ cup butter, softened at room temperature

4 cups powdered sugar

4 teaspoons vanilla extract

Tools

Measuring cups

Measuring spoons

Electric or hand mixer

Mixing bowl

Spreader or rubber spatula

Instructions

1. Place the cream cheese and butter in a mixing bowl and beat with an electric mixer on low to medium speed for 30 seconds.

2. Add the powdered sugar and vanilla and continue to beat for one minute or until frosting is smooth and creamy.

3. Place one cake layer on a cake plate. Top with about 1 cup of frosting and spread all over the top of the cake with a spreader or rubber spatula. Place the second cake layer on top. Top with another cup of frosting and spread all over the top. Use more frosting if needed to cover the cakes completely. Cover the sides of the cake completely with the remaining frosting, and use the spreader or spatula to smooth out the sides.

4. Decorate with your favorite cake toppings. Try sliced strawberries or other fresh fruit!

Tres Leches (Milk Cake)

Tres Leches Cake

Ingredients

1 ½ cups all-purpose flour

1 teaspoon baking powder

½ cup unsalted butter (1 stick), softened at room temperature

¾ cup cup granulated sugar

5 eggs

½ teaspoon vanilla extract

1 cup whole milk

6 ounces (½ can) sweetened condensed milk

6 ounces (½ can) evaporated milk

Tools

9 x 13-inch baking pan

2 large bowls

Sifter

Wooden spoon

Electric or hand mixer

Fork

Measuring cups

Measuring spoons

Whisk

Alternative

Decorate the top of the cake with shredded coconut and sliced strawberries.

Instructions

1. Preheat oven to 350 degrees. Grease the baking pan with butter, then sprinkle flour in the pan and tap the sides to spread it around evenly.

2. Sift the flour and baking powder together into a large bowl and set aside.

3. Place the butter and sugar in a large bowl and mix with the wooden spoon. Add the eggs and vanilla extract and beat together with the hand mixer or electric mixer until the mixture is fluffy.

4. Add the flour mixture to the butter and egg mixture little by little, mixing after each addition to combine. When the flour mixture is fully combined, pour the batter into the pan.

5. Bake for 30 minutes and remove from the oven carefully using oven mitts. Pierce the cake with a fork all over (every inch or so), all the way to the bottom of the pan.

6. Whisk the whole milk, condensed milk, and evaporated milk together in a large bowl. When the cake cools, pour the milk mixture over the top. Spread with frosting.

Whipped Frosting

(Makes about 4 Cups)

Ingredients

1 cup heavy whipping cream

2 tablespoons granulated sugar

½ teaspoon vanilla extract

Tools

Measuring cups

Measuring spoons

Large bowl

Instructions

1. Place the cream, sugar, and vanilla together in a bowl and beat with an electric mixer until thick and smooth.

2. Spread over the top of cake. Refrigerate for at least three hours before serving.

Dutch Apple Crisp

Level

Ingredients

5 large apples, cored, peeled and chopped into bite-sized pieces

1 cup agave nectar or honey, divided

2 tablespoons lemon juice

1 teaspoon vanilla extract

1 cup oats

½ cup whole wheat pastry flour

1 teaspoon cinnamon

½ teaspoon salt

¼ cup unsalted butter, cubed

Tools

Cutting board

Knife

Measuring cups

Measuring spoons

2 large bowls

Wooden spoon

9-inch square baking pan

Instructions

1. Preheat oven to 375 degrees. Lightly grease baking pan with butter or cooking spray.

2. In large bowl, combine apples, lemon juice, vanilla and ½ cup of agave nectar or honey. Pour into baking pan.

3. In a separate bowl, combine oats, flour, cinnamon, salt and butter. Mix the butter in with your hands to make a coarse, crumbly mixture.

4. Pour remaining ½ cup agave nectar or honey over oat mixture and spread evenly over apples.

5. Bake for 30 minutes until top is golden-brown. Cool for 15 minutes and serve.

Alternative

Use a pre-made pie crust in place of a baking pan to make an apple pie. Serve with a scoop of vanilla ice cream!

Sweet Treats from Across the Globe

Oh my, it's a Whoopie Pie

Whoopie Pies

Ingredients

½ cup (1 stick) unsalted butter, softened at room temperature

1 cup granulated sugar

1 egg

1 ½ teaspoons baking soda

½ teaspoon baking powder

1 teaspoon vanilla extract

½ cup unsweetened cocoa powder

1 cup milk

2 cups all-purpose flour

Tools

Measuring cups

Measuring spoons

Large bowl

Electric or hand mixer

Spoon

Parchment paper

Baking sheet

Alternative

Instead of frosting, use your favorite ice cream to make a whoopie ice cream pie.

Instructions

1. Preheat the oven to 350 degrees. Place the butter and sugar in a large bowl and beat with an electric mixer on medium speed until smooth and fluffy.

2. Add the egg and mix until combined.

3. Add the baking soda, baking powder, vanilla extract and cocoa powder. Mix on low speed until combined.

4. Add the milk and flour. Mix on low speed until the batter is smooth.

5. Lay out the parchment paper on the baking sheet.

6. Spoon the batter onto the baking sheet into little round pancakes. Each pancake should be less than 2 inches across, and there should be 3 inches between each pancake because the batter will expand as it bakes. Smooth out the top of the pancakes with the back of the spoon.

7. Bake for 15 minutes, then remove and let cool completely. Make whoopie pie sandwiches with Cream Cheese Frosting in the middle.

Cream Cheese Frosting

Ingredients

1 cup cream cheese, softened at room temperature

½ cup unsalted butter (1 stick), softened at room temperature

½ cup powdered sugar

1 teaspoon vanilla

Tools

Measuring cups

Measuring spoons

Large bowl

Electric or hand mixer

Spreading knife

Instructions

1. Place all the ingredients in a bowl and beat with an electric mixer on medium to high speed until fluffy.

2. Spread frosting on one pancake, sandwich with a second pancake, and serve!

South African Pumpkin Bread Pudding

South African Pumpkin Bread Pudding

Ingredients

- slices white bread
- cup half and half
- cup canned
  100% pumpkin puree
- eggs
- teaspoon vanilla
- cup granulated sugar
- cup dark brown sugar
- teaspoon salt
- teaspoon cinnamon
- teaspoon pumpkin pie spice

Tools

- Measuring cups
- Measuring spoons
- Whisk
- Medium bowl
- Large mixing bowl
- Rubber spatula
- Large metal scoop
- Silicone baking cups

Instructions

1. Preheat oven to 350 degrees.
2. Tear the bread into bite-sized pieces. Place in a bowl and set aside.
3. Place the canned pumpkin, half and half, eggs and vanilla in the large bowl and whisk to combine.
4. Add the granulated and brown sugar, salt, cinnamon and pumpkin pie spice. Whisk until the mixture is smooth.
5. Gently fold in the bread pieces using a rubber spatula.
6. Put the mixture in the refrigerator for at least 1 hour.
7. Spray the silicone baking cups with nonstick cooking spray. Spoon the mixture into baking cups.
8. Bake in the oven for 25 minutes and remove carefully with oven mitts. Top with Brown Sugar Sauce.

Brown Sugar Sauce

Ingredients

1 ¼ cup dark brown sugar

½ cup heavy cream

½ cup (1 stick) unsalted butter

Tools

Measuring cups

Medium saucepan

Wooden spoon

Instructions

1. Place brown sugar and butter in a saucepan on the stovetop over medium heat. Stir with a wooden spoon until the butter is melted.
2. Add the cream and stir until the sugar dissolves and the sauce is smooth (about 3 minutes).
3. Turn off the heat, and let the sauce sit for a few minutes. Pour over bread pudding and serve!

Alternative

Make one large bread pudding instead of individual bread puddings. Spread a thin coating of butter on the bottom and sides of an 8-inch baking pan. Pour the mixture into the pan and bake for about 35 minutes, then top with Brown Sugar Sauce.

Makes: About 12 Bars

Ingredients

- ½ cup all-purpose flour
- ½ cup whole wheat flour
- ¼ cup brown sugar
- ½ teaspoon cinnamon
- ⅛ teaspoon salt
- ½ cup (1 stick) cold unsalted butter
- 2 cups pitted dried dates
- ⅓ cup boiling water
- ¼ cup walnut pieces

Tools

- 8-inch square baking pan
- Paper towel
- Large bowl
- Whisk
- Butter knife
- Cutting board
- Medium bowl

Alternative

Try using other kinds of dried fruit and a handful of chocolate chips.

Instructions

1. Preheat the oven to 350 degrees. Grease the baking pan lightly with butter.

2. Combine the all-purpose flour, whole wheat flour, brown sugar, cinnamon and salt in the large bowl. Whisk together.

3. Cut the butter into chunks with a knife. Use your fingertips to mix the butter with the flour mixture until it is combined but still crumbly.

4. Place ⅔ of the flour mixture in the baking pan, and pat down firmly all along the bottom of the pan to make a crust.

5. Slice the dates and put them in the medium bowl. Add boiling water. Wait until the water is cool enough to touch, then use your hands to mix the dates with the water until it forms a squishy paste. Add the walnuts and mix together.

6. Carefully spread the date mixture in the baking pan evenly on top of the crust.

7. Sprinkle the remaining ⅓ of the flour mixture on top of the date layer.

8. Bake for about 30 minutes until the top is browned. Let cool, cut into squares, and serve!

French Pots de Crème

ngredients

- ½ cups half and half
- teaspoon vanilla extract
- large eggs
- cup sugar
- inch of salt
- ounces semi-sweet chocolate chips

ools

- Measuring cups
- Measuring spoons
- Kettle
- small microwave-safe bowls
- Medium bowl
- Medium saucepan
- Wooden spoon
- Whisk
- Ramekins, custard cups, or small oven-safe bowls
- Baking pan
- Aluminum foil

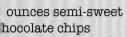

Alternative

Bake the pots in oven-safe mugs to make it look like hot chocolate. Then add a little whipped cream on top.

Instructions

1. Preheat oven to 325 degrees. Bring a kettle of water to a boil.

2. Separate the egg yolks from the whites: lightly crack the egg over a small bowl and very gently let just the whites drip into the bowl. Shift the yolk back and forth between the two halves of the eggshell or your hands while the whites drip into the small bowl. Place the egg yolks in a medium bowl. Save the egg whites for another use or discard.

3. Add sugar and salt to the bowl with the egg yolks and beat with a whisk until combined.

4. Melt the chocolate chips in a small bowl in the microwave, 30 seconds at a time, stirring until smooth. Pour the melted chocolate in the bowl with the egg yolks and whisk to combine.

5. Place half and half and vanilla in a medium saucepan and heat until it begins to bubble, then remove from the heat.

6. Slowly add the hot half and half to the bowl, whisking constantly. It will get foamy as you whisk—use a spoon to skim the foam off the surface.

7. Place four small ramekins or oven-safe bowls in a baking pan. Divide the chocolate mixture evenly among the ramekins. Then carefully pour some hot water from the kettle around the ramekins into the baking pan, just until it comes halfway up the sides of the ramekins.

8. Place the baking pan in the oven carefully using oven mitts and lay a piece of aluminum foil on top. Bake 40-45 minutes, until the chocolate is set but slightly jiggly.

9. Carefully remove the baking pan using oven mitts. Chill the ramekins in the refrigerator for 2 hours before serving.